The
Christmas
Apron

OTHER BOOKS AND AUDIO BOOKS
BY RACHELLE PACE CASTOR:

Eliza's Field of Faith

The Christmas Apron

Rachelle Pace Castor

Covenant Communications, Inc.

For my sisters

Published by Covenant Communications, Inc.
American Fork, Utah

Printed in The United States of America
First Printing: October 2010

16 15 14 13 12 11 10   10 9 8 7 6 5 4 3 2 1

ISBN-13: 978-1-60861-092-1

*D*ecember 1942 the snows fell early and deep in our town. The drifts banked so high we could slide right out our second-story windows into soft, powdery bliss. Every chance we got, we children flopped into an untouched spot to make snow angels—*angelic signatures,* Dad called them. We had signed heaven's name all over our little town.

The freezing cold kept the snow fluffy for days and the tiniest puff of wind would sweep the silvery flakes up in a flurry of glitter. My eleven-year-old heart was lit up with the magical feeling that all Christmas dreams were sure to come true.

Just a week before Christmas an unexpected announcement came at the end of dance class. I was unpinning my long, dark braids when Mistress Allen tapped her stick on the ground.

"Attention girls, attention. I have an announcement since we won't meet again until after Christmas break." She looked at me. "Miss Mildred, step forward please."

I did so with hesitation.

"Don't look so terrified, dear," she said. But I was terrified. I couldn't imagine what she had called me out for. Mistress Allen never complimented her dancers. I braced myself for a public rebuke. Then she put her arm around my shoulders. "I want the entire class to know that you, Miss Mildred, are ready to dance en pointe."

I nearly stopped breathing, with my hands pressed to my face, eyes wide. The other girls gathered around me, patting my back. *Oh, Millie. Congratulations Millie. How wonderful for you, Millie. I wish my point was as lovely as yours, Millie.*

My long-awaited dream of pink, silky pointe shoes came with a grand jeté into my mind. I gulped in a bit of air. "Really?" was all that came out. "Really?" I was certain I would go on smiling through eternity if I didn't faint first. I tried not to look as proud as I felt.

I was so elated that what Mistress Allen said next didn't phase me. "Of course, pointe shoes are nearly impossible to find with the war shortages."

I was still smiling.

"If by some miracle you can get into a pair before the New Year, you're certain to be ready to perform in *The Nutcracker* by *next* Christmas."

The Nutcracker! I floated home, a believer.

* * *

Hoping to tell Mom first, I burst in the door only to have my sister Grace, two years younger than me, tell me with a little smirk that Mom and Dad were "planning."

No problem. I could wait. I felt like my feet didn't touch the ground as I helped the twins, Winnie and Will, set our large oval dining table. Smells of stew and baking biscuits filled the air. Not even the silly, never-ending seven-year-old games the twins played could bother me tonight. As they raced around the table placing plates, cups, and silverware, they chanted out each family member's name at their assigned seat.

"Mom . . . Dad . . . Millie . . . Grace . . . Winnie . . . Will . . . Dottie . . . Preston . . . Georgie . . . Jimmy . . ."

"Hey you two, take Jimmy's off. He's at *his* house tonight," I said. Scruffy little freckle-faced Jimmy Gordon was with us so much it seemed he should have a regular place. It didn't bother me. Mom said if anybody deserved a break, Jimmy did. Our dad was lucky enough to be needed at a war factory here at home. Jimmy's dad was unlucky enough to be over there fighting while Jimmy's mother raised six children alone. Jimmy got more attention—and more food—at our house. He was just one of us.

Will and Winnie finished the table and ran off. *Redheads,* I thought. Still smiling.

Eager to tell Mom and Dad my fabulous news, I grabbed the stack of towels I'd just folded and bounded upstairs, went to the closet at the end of the hall, placed them inside, then turned to wait by my folks' room, empty arms now rounded high in fifth position, face still beaming.

Mom and Dad's bedroom door was ajar. I should have left the minute I heard Dad's tone. His words slipped out and hit me so hard the breath went out of me like when I land belly first in the community pool.

"None. Not a spare nickel for gifts this year, honey. Even if there were, where would we ever find what the children are hoping for?"

Mom's voice sounded quivery. "No money for Christmas? But Denny . . . Denny! Not even for the little ones? This isn't right. The children have gone without so much—you at the factory nonstop and now with their Grandpa serving over seas."

"I know, I know. Everything seems swallowed up in the war effort—same as every town in the country."

I stood stiff and still. My arms dropped as my smile wilted. From the dark hall I could see Mom through the crack of the door. Her chin lifted just so, her eyes filling with tears. A heavy feeling came into my heart—sadness, hurt, and anger, all mixed together. It sent a cold shiver right to my bones. The pointe shoe vision began to fade. I wanted to pretend I hadn't heard, or throw something—or both.

Little Georgie started to bawl across the house. I dashed away to quiet him, my breath held tight, wiping tears as I ran fast down the stairs on my silent dancer feet.

The secret worried me through dinner. Mom and Dad went on like everything was normal, questioning us about school. They smiled and laughed at little Georgie as he dipped his biscuit in stew and sucked it off. I didn't join in. I couldn't stop thinking about the disappointment Christmas morning would bring to me and my six little siblings. I would do just about anything for them. Why did I have to be the oldest?

As dinner ended Mom said, "Millie, will you play mom? Grace and I need to rehearse at the church tonight."

"Sure." I faked a smile as they bundled up and left.

I cleaned Georgie with a dishrag and lifted him out of his high chair. He wouldn't even notice the lack of presents. But the others . . .

Preston, my three-year-old brother, got to help me with dish duty. As we worked, I thought about how he'd told me every day since his birthday, "My puppy couldn't find my birthday but he will find my Christmas." While he was stacking the last spoon in the drawer, I mussed his dark curls. When he grinned up at me, I couldn't imagine him not getting that puppy.

Dottie came into the kitchen then, paint smeared on her face and long dark curls hanging to her waist.

"I did one more painting—pleeease help me hang it, Millie." She was bouncing on her heels.

"I don't know where we can," I said. "You've filled every bit of wall space."

"There," she pointed. We rearranged her other art to make room on the kitchen wall.

"Beautiful," I said at the still damp whatever-it-was.

"I'm out of paints!" she said, squeezing her cheeks in her little hands.

I cringed as she ran off to bed, Mom's words echoing in my head. *Not even enough for the little ones.*

"Winnie, Will, bedtime you two!" Dad hollered down to the twins.

Nobody could tell our twins were twins because at seven, Will was already a head taller than Winnie. Tugging and pulling each other back to be the first to reach Dad, they started up the stairs.

Without thinking I blurted out, "Hey, you two better behave if you want presents for . . ." Winnie turned and stuck out her tongue.

In a flash my worry turned to anger. I hated this. Why had I overheard my parents? The smile I thought would never leave my face was gone. What was happening to me? Grace would be home any minute, and sharing a bedroom with her would drive me crazy again tonight. "Princess Grace," I called her. Our family royalty even though she was only nine. She had that look—the only one of us with nearly pure white hair—soft curls to her shoulders—and green eyes instead of brown like the rest of us. *I need to shake this feeling before I have to deal with Grace,* I thought.

Too late. Grace rushed in, breathless from rehearsal. "Beat you upstairs!"

"I'm not playing your dumb games," I said.

"Fine." She raced off, nose in the air. "I'm telling Mom you called me dumb."

I closed my eyes and took a deep breath. Mom came in with a blast of cold air. *Should I say something?* Her question came first.

"You okay, sweetie?"

I opened my eyes and pasted on a smile. "Sure," I said as I untied my apron. It was then, with my apron in my hands, that a bright beam of light flicked on in my head and spread across the dark fog of my worries. My heart tingled, like when your foot starts to wake up from sitting on it too long.

Gramma! I thought. *Gramma will be here tomorrow. She'll bring the Christmas apron. Gramma will fix everything.*

"Thanks for your help." Mom's voice jarred me. "I can always count on my Millie."

With a little help from Gramma, maybe she was right.

* * *

When I got to our room, Grace was already in our shared double bed. I didn't care that she had beat me there. My usual routine was to practice a hundred changements—beginning in fifth position, jumping up and landing with the other foot in front, back and forth with pointed toes, of course, and staying in the air as long as possible to keep my amazing feet off the cold wood floor. It was great practice to increase my elevation and suspension, and it warmed me up on winter nights. With new hope for Gramma to save the day, I pulled on my red-striped flannel nightgown, did all one hundred jumps, and then slid in next to Grace. We yanked the quilt up over our heads to keep our warm breath and whispering under cover.

"I'm freezing." Princess Grace began her usual complaining. "Remember how Gramma used to put warm rocks from the fireplace in the bed to warm it up? Let's have her show us how to do that when she comes tomorrow."

I ignored her, hoping she'd fall asleep so I could fantasize about how Gramma was going to fix everything. It didn't work.

"I can't wait till tomorrow," said Grace. "What's your Christmas apron wish, Millie?"

A little flare of irritation flashed inside me, and I clamped my jaw. Grace had a way of making me talk even when I was determined not to. I was not going to let the no-money secret out. And she would never know about the pointe shoes.

But Grace wouldn't stop. "Millie! I *said,* what's your Christmas apron wish?"

Even in the under-the-cover darkness I could feel those flashing green eyes staring at me, so I finally answered. "My wish is private this year." I turned away, hoping to stay true to my vow of silence.

"No fair, Mill! We've always shared our apron wishes."

I sighed. "Forget it, Princess Grace!"

"It doesn't matter," she said. "I already know what you want. I heard it from your dance classmate Mary Lou. Pointe shoes."

My face flushed. I hit my fist into the soft mattress. The hopeless feeling returned.

"Does everybody in this town have to know everybody else's business? For your information, it's a wish that will never go in the apron pocket because it's too expensive," I said without thinking. Too late.

Now Grace hit her fist into the mattress. "Mildred Rose! You think I don't know Christmas is going to be different this year? There *is* a war going on, if you hadn't noticed!"

She was brighter than I wanted to admit.

"But we can still share our wishes. Besides," she said, her voice calm now, "this is just a wish. I know Gramma's apron isn't really magical. But I want to pretend just one more year."

"You didn't tell Mom what Mary Lou said, did you?"

She shook her head.

"Good. Promise you won't tell about the pointe shoes, Grace. It's a secret you have to keep locked away. Promise?"

"Cross my heart," said Grace, and she drew her finger across her chest with a nod, her white curls shiny even in the under-the-cover shadows.

"Pointe shoes," she said again, kind of dreamy. My feet warmed at her words.

"It's a wonderful wish, Millie. And if anybody deserves it, you do. I'm sorry about the war shortages."

I kept my silence. How could I be mad when she seemed to want the best for me?

"But if *your* wish is too expensive, my wish is *way* too expensive for the Christmas apron."

"You still have to tell now that you know my wish," I said.

Clearing her throat, she put on her theater voice. "If I could have anything in the world . . . I'd wish for . . ." Her voice went soft, almost reverent. "I'd wish for . . . for a horse."

My heart sank.

"A horse? Impossible, Grace."

But that didn't stop her. She went right on wishing in that little sing-songy voice of hers and my irritation at my ditzy little sister was back.

"Just think, Mill, every day I'd run home from school. My horse would perk up her ears at the sight of me. She'd gallop to me and whinny, like she was calling my name . . . 'Gracie, Gracie.' I'd open the gate to the pasture—"

"We live in town," I said.

She didn't take a breath.

"*My* very own horse. I'd curry her shiny coat and long mane and extra-long-to-the-ground tail, then climb on her back and ride like in the fairy tales, the wind blowing my hair." Her voice wavered at the end.

Was she crying?

I couldn't believe what I'd just heard. I felt heavy and kind of sick to my stomach. Was it her sappy fantasy, or the knowledge that her wish would never come true? Holding my breath, I stayed still, hoping Grace had fallen asleep. Then gently, I pulled back the quilt. The moonlight streaming through the window fell on her princess face. Eyes closed, wistful smile, her whole face was beaming, but a single tear ran into her white curls.

That darn tear. My little sister's wish was a whole-soul wish. I should have known. Little snatches of clues—telltale signs of Grace's wish—came to mind. The past few weeks her every spare minute had been spent reading horse stories and sketching their proud heads.

As her breathing grew deep and rhythmic, I curled up into a ball, unable to stop worrying that even Gramma's Christmas apron couldn't make this wish come true. The cold-to-the-bone feeling was back. I made up my mind to ease my parents' burden by making my own wish something simple, like a book or a pair of Gramma's mittens. But that didn't seem to settle right either. I tossed and turned all night.

* * *

When morning came I was so tired. Thank heavens the last day of school before Christmas break was a party day and we got out early, otherwise I wouldn't have made it through the afternoon without getting in trouble for falling asleep during a lesson. At last we were on our way home, sticking together as family—with Jimmy Gordon tucked inside our bunch, of course—but run-walking to be the first to see Gramma.

I wanted like crazy to race ahead and welcome Gramma first. Maybe I could tell her the crummy secret before the others got to her. But, as always, I found myself needing to help the little ones.

"Millie, my bag is too heavy." Dottie was carrying a big, old brown grocery bag, the top rolled down, but otherwise bulging. I didn't want to stop and help, but of course I did.

"Mrs. Spencer made me clean out my desk and bring all my art home for Christmas break! I don't like being in first grade." She looked so pathetic standing there, her cheeks bright red from the cold, her long dark curls tumbling out of her light blue hood and her mittenless hands too frozen to grasp the bulky bag any longer.

"Where are your mittens, Dot?" I asked. Her lip stuck out farther.

"Maybe you should have thrown some of your art away," I scolded. Her face was stricken. All hope to get to Gramma first dissolved. And then, dummy me, my long night of worry seemed to come bursting out. "There's not room in the whole world for all your art, Dottie." I was looking around for Grace. Why was it always the oldest stuck taking care of everyone?

Tears formed in Dottie's eyes. She blurted out, "I'm telling Mom you hate my artwork!"

I felt lousy. I could hear what Gramma would say. *There's always time to be kind, Millie.*

I took a breath and knelt down on the sidewalk in front of her. "I do not hate your artwork, Dottie." The icy snow bit at my bare knee as I hoisted her bag under my free arm. My voice softened. "Listen, honey," I said, sounding like Mom. "I'm sure when we get home Gramma is going to be so glad you brought home every single project for her to see."

Dottie's face spread into a grin. She raced away shouting, "Gramma, Gramma, wait till you see what I brought you!" I stood alone, feeling forgotten on the frozen sidewalk, bitter wind blowing snow against me. *Just great.* I was holding the "what" Dottie wanted Gramma to see, so I pushed past the cold and my over-packed arms and ran to catch up with the others.

As we turned the corner, we saw Gramma's green Studebaker, and broke loose—running our fastest—and shouting together, "Did you bring it? Did you bring it?"

Gramma met us on the porch, holding baby Georgie on her hip and one-arm-hugging us. She kissed us each on the head. She even kissed Jimmy Gordon.

"Did you bring it?" we all said again.

"Yes, yes, of course! It's a bit faded for all its years. But it's here and ready to do its magic!" She looked right at me and raised one eyebrow. My frustration melted. Gramma was here.

We rushed inside, dropping books and lunch pails and a bag full of art projects. Gathering around the bed in the guest room, we waited as breathless and still as our frozen angels that lay all over town. Mom came in with Preston to join in the moment.

"Millie, Millie." My heart melted at the sound of my brother's three-year-old voice as he climbed on my lap. Mom took baby Georgie from Gramma so Gramma could get to her suitcase. With Mom and her mom standing next to each other, I could see how alike they were, even though Gramma's hair was now silver white. I longed to be like them.

The room went silent. Ever so slowly Gramma opened her suitcase. There on top was the Christmas apron, worn but crisp, clean, and filled with the magical memories of generations of Christmas wishes come true. At the sight of it, there was a wave of giddy giggling and bouncing; I was the only one who was still.

Gramma cleared her throat to get our attention. Even though she was a country girl, her beautiful hair pulled up in a French twist gave her a graceful, almost royal, appearance and, though I hated to admit it, I could see where Grace got her princess looks.

Gramma began, "This very apron has helped our family through many a hard time," she said. "It's wiped the tears from all our faces, shooed away unwelcome chickens from the kitchen, and carried in tomatoes, apples, and new puppies from the early frosts." Preston pulled his slobbery pointer finger out of his mouth long enough to yelp twice at the word *puppy*. Gramma tweaked his nose. "And it's the last thing to be seen by those we love when we wave our goodbye with it from the porch."

"Don't forget," said Will, his red hair wild from having just pulled off his snow hat, "it makes our Christmas wishes come true! Like Lincoln L—"

Winnie slapped her hand over his mouth. "No telling," she said. "You'll break the rules and never get your wish!"

Grace and I caught each other's glance as if to assure our secret wish-telling was safe between us.

"That was a close one," Gramma said to Will. "What do you say to your sister?"

"Thanks, Winnie," he said, his face almost as red as his hair.

"I like what you said, Will. It's very close to the truth. The apron *helps* our wishes come true. That it does."

He smiled and nodded, his freckles shiny.

"Now, listen carefully to your grandmother," she went on, looking into each of our eyes in turn. "The apron will hang near the fireplace for one day—no later than bedtime tomorrow night—at which point there will only be three days left before Christmas, so don't be tardy. In the meantime, our Christmas apron is not to be used to keep my dress clean, or wipe my floury hands on, or even to rub the steam from the windows so I can watch your snowball fights. It's here for one purpose—to collect the Christmas wishes of my grandchildren."

Jimmy Gordon let out a sad sigh, and Gramma ruffled his sandy hair till he grinned. "This apron has a way of inspiring love all around, Jimmy." His face wrinkled with a look like he was thinking real hard about that.

"Now remember," she said, "only one wish. Choose wisely."

With a burst of excitement, Grace, Winnie, and Will ran to write their wishes.

"I'll help the pre-writers." Mom hoisted Georgie and shooed Preston off to the kitchen. "Come on Jimmy, let's get you a piece of bread and jam," she said.

Jimmy dashed away with the rest, but I stayed on Gramma's bed.

As the room quieted, I found that *I* couldn't keep quiet one more minute.

"Gramma, I don't think I can wait till Christmas Eve to hear the story. Would you tell me now?"

"Of course I'll tell you." She pushed the suitcase over and sat down by me, pulling her blue sweater with white snowflakes knitted right in tight around her. "You seem anxious, Millie."

"I'm just a little worried for Mom and Dad. I'm old enough to know that Christmas costs money." The whole truth of the secret seemed stuck in my throat.

"You're growing up, Millie. I remember last Christmas you were focused solely on your own wish, which is how it should be for little ones." Her head bobbed, emphasizing each word. "Christmas isn't about what's happening around us. It's about what's on the inside. And I think Christmas is happening inside you, Millie girl." She cupped her hand so gently on my cheek I felt sure I would cry, but I forced a smile.

"This story always seems to help when I'm not feeling sure of things," Gramma said. "And with your Grandpa being career military and off to war, I need to hear this story, too." She held the apron in her lap like a book and began.

* * *

On their wedding day, Jed said to Josie, "Let's move to the open country where we can raise our family away from the world, close to God, and close to each other."

"That's what matters most," Josie said.

So they gave up city living, sold most everything they owned, packed the wagon, and headed to the sea of red grasses known as the prairie lands.

Their little sod house wasn't much more than earth and stones stacked tight together, so Josie went to work making it a home. She cut and sewed and cut and sewed till she turned all her fancy city dresses into quilts and curtains, dishtowels and hot pads.

The last few scraps she sewed together with ruffles and bows that made a pretty little apron, strangely fancy for a prairie wife.

When Jed saw the apron for the first time he looked a bit dismayed.

"Jed," said Josie, "it's an apron. And it's my daily reminder that we gave up fancy things for things that matter."

"I see," said Jed with a smile.

"And," Josie said in her reminding voice, "Gramma always said aprons help us do the most important work there is—family work. The work that says 'I love you.'"

And that's just what happened. Each day Josie's apron performed its many tasks. It gave her a place to wipe her floury hands when baking buttermilk biscuits for dinner. It brought in vegetables from the garden, wood from the woodpile, and on chilly nights, new puppies from the barn to sleep warm by the fire.

It was the symbol of family Jed looked back to see each morning as Josie waved it high from the porch when he left for the fields. And it was the signal that called him back when supper was on the table. It kept Josie's dress clean so unexpected guests could be welcomed in a respectable manner. It wiped the steamy window so she could look out on her beloved sea of grass, and shooed away unwelcome chickens from the kitchen. Josie's apron was busy every day of every season—spring, summer, autumn. Then came winter. By now the apron just barely covered Josie's swollen tummy, pointing to the fact that their family would be growing—soon.

The day before Christmas Jed said, "We've run low on supplies sooner than I planned. I'll take the wagon to town and be back by suppertime. Don't let that baby come without me."

Josie watched her Jed, dressed in his red wool jacket and cap, drive off toward the red sky of morning through a sea of red grass now stiff from the cold, dry winds. "Hmmm," Josie mused to no one but the chickens. "Red, on red, on red. Strange—almost like a warning."

Sure enough, the wind blew up a storm, and snow began dumping so fast the prairie farmers would tell stories for years to come, calling it "the year the sky cracked."

With such a blizzard and Jed gone to town, Josie knew someone must check on the animals. She bundled up and found that Ol' Gal, the milk cow, had been frightened by the blizzard, kicked through the gate, and wandered off. Josie knew Ol' Gal would die in such weather, and a prairie wife's animals are almost as important as people for keeping a family alive. So she followed Ol' Gal's tracks right into the side of a cliff. As luck would have it Ol' Gal was bellowing louder than the storm. Josie pushed back a prairie bush and found the frightened cow in a hidden cave.

"Well," said Josie as she pondered what to do. "One thing's for certain—I know this baby isn't going to wait. And the snow's coming down as thick as whipped meringue—it's already covered our tracks. My sea of red is now a sea of white. We'll never find our way back home. And when Jed comes searching, he'll never find us in our hideaway."

So, with a wisdom she felt sure came straight from her now-angel grandmother, she took off her apron, tied it high and tight to the bush outside, made herself as comfortable as possible, and prayed out loud her Christmas wish. "Please, dear Father in Heaven, help us bring this baby here safely." It was a whole-soul wish.

Jed got home and found their little house empty. Seeing the broken gate, he knew just what had happened and took Pal, still pulling the wagon, out searching. There was nothing but snow as far as the eye could see.

"Why, this snow is nearly up to Pal's knee bones. What matters most might be lost for good." As Jed worried over his wife and baby so soon to be born, he tried to decide which way to go. Everything was white—white mule against white grass against white sky—white, on white, on white. So, without even knowing, he prayed the same Christmas wish his Josie had prayed. "Please God, help us bring this baby here safely." His, too, was a whole-soul wish.

Jed searched again and again, hand held to his furrowed brow, shielding his squinting eyes from the brightness of the white on white on white, hoping for a sign, and believing.

As the wind grew louder and the snow grew deeper, Jed was nearly blinded. He pressed Pal to move on. He prayed. Then off in the distance he caught a flash of color waving in the wind.

"It's Josie's apron!" he whooped to Pal.

Jed arrived at the cave just in time to catch that baby and wrap her up in an apron used for the most important work—family work. The little family spent their first Christmas in a cave . . . Mommy, Daddy, Ol' Gal, Pal the mule, and—

"And you, Gramma." I interrupted to tell my favorite part. "You were that new baby. Do you really think the apron made the Christmas wish come true?"

Gramma smiled. "Well, we didn't get a thing from Santa that year. Our gift was straight from heaven. The apron doesn't have any special power, Millie, but it became a family symbol for us. Aprons help us do the most important work there is—family work. The work that says 'I love you.'"

Gramma and I sat for a time in silence. I wanted so much to share the secret, but the words wouldn't come. Besides, I had always believed in Gramma's Christmas apron. This year I would need to believe a little more.

* * *

I slept well that night. My dreams were filled with colorful aprons flapping in a great snowstorm. And I woke up smiling, with a new hope in my heart. Down the stairs I danced, pirouetting three times as I entered the kitchen.

"There's our girl," said Gramma. "Your dad's already off to

the factory, and your mother and I have packed up a basketful of Christmas from the pantry and icebox."

I surveyed it, pretty as a picture. Nestled together were two roasting hens, a bag of potatoes, jams and marmalade, and a bottle of each kind of fruit and vegetable we'd canned the previous year. Wait. An anxious feeling welled up inside me as it all fell into place in my mind. Lying on top of the food were lots of mittens—Gramma had knitted at least a half dozen sets—and . . . a pair of silk stockings. My eyes grew wide at the sight of those. I knew Mom had been saving those silk stockings for something special now that they were impossible to buy anywhere because of the war.

"The basket is ready for a secret drop off at the Gordons'," said Mom. She was bent over the big kitchen table rolling biscuit dough. "You and Grace go together this year."

I was still staring at the large basket, not really listening. Dad's words kept sounding in my head over and over. *Not a spare nickel, not even for the little ones.* My frustration finally came blurting out. "But Mom, we barely have enough for our own family." The anger in my voice surprised even me.

She stopped mid-roll and scowled up at me. "Millie! What's gotten into you? When someone's in need, we all pitch in. Remember the loaves and fishes? There will be enough. The Lord counts on us to pass around the blessings."

I looked at Gramma and the loving lift of one eyebrow seemed to sweeten my bitter tongue.

"Sorry, Mom," seemed the only thing to say. "We'll go right away."

"Dress warm," she reminded me.

I did, and so did Grace. The only problem was she came into the kitchen dressed as her most dramatic princess self. She'd found one of Gramma's old rabbit-fur hats, a white one that the little ones used for dressing up. Her white curls blended into the white fur, and she had white socks on her hands for mittens and a white wool blanket draped over her shoulders.

"Camouflage," she said to my puzzled look.

"Right." I decided not to argue.

The morning sun had tinted the neighborhood pale lavender as Grace and I pulled the sled down the streets and around the massive drifts of snow to the edge of town where country cottages stood nestled deep into the snow-blanketed meadows.

As we walked, Grace would occasionally stop, let go of the sled's rope, and squeal, "Ooh! Another perfect spot for a snow angel." Then she'd take off the blanket, lie down ever so carefully and move her arms up and down, her legs in and out, in the perfect angel pattern.

I continued to walk ahead, irritated to be pulling the sleigh alone, mumbling a little. It's not that I wasn't glad she was enjoying herself and glad for the angels. What she didn't seem to have a clue about was how much I would love to be playing like she was. I could practice the grand jeté sequence of split-legged leaps we were learning for *Swan Lake,* arms held high in front in joyful freedom. But we did have a job to do. All Grace seemed to be thinking about were her angels. "Seven," she said as she finished another just half a block from the Gordons', white blanket flapping behind her as she ran to catch up. "One for each of us kids. I just know these angels are going to bring our family good luck."

"All right, Grace," I whispered. "Stop goofing off. It's time to get serious. Remember—quiet, sneaking steps to the porch, knock, and then RUN!"

"Got it," said Grace, putting on her serious face as she re-cloaked herself in the blanket.

We did as we planned: placed the basket, knocked loudly, then turned and dashed away, sled bouncing behind us.

As we sprinted over the snow I strained a whisper. "Back behind this bush!" As I dove for cover, Grace didn't. I looked back to see what had happened. She had stopped halfway, standing in plain view.

"Grace! Get over here," I warned. But the princess didn't budge. "Grace!"

Nothing. Frustrated, I packed a snowball tight and hard and heaved it, hitting her in the shoulder just as the Gordons' door opened with shouts of delight. Still Grace didn't move. After pulling the basket inside, Jimmy turned, grinned, made giant arm waves of gratitude, then closed the door.

I stood and put my hands on my hips. "What are you thinking?" I said. "It was supposed to be a secret surprise. They weren't supposed to know it's from us!"

Grace turned but wouldn't look at me.

"I'm sorry, Mill," she said, sounding like a wounded bird.

Still furious I said, "I don't accept your apology. You've ruined everything!"

"But Mill, I just had . . . I just had to see their faces when they saw the gifts." She closed her eyes and lifted her face toward the morning sun, her white hair, hat, and blanket blending into the snow. "And Millie, it was . . . it was glorious! I wish you could have seen too."

Just then a breath of wind caught the snow and swirled it all around my little sister, each flake catching a drop of the thin morning sun, glittering and sparkling in a whirl of crystal.

White, on white, on white.

My anger vanished as Gramma's words came into my mind. *Christmas isn't about what's happening all around us. It's about what's happening on the inside.* And Grace was being *my* example—the little twit.

We walked home in silence, pulling the empty sled behind us.

* * *

The rest of the day passed in a blur. Gramma kept us all busy doing Christmas fun, and the house had a warm peace that I needed. Grace stayed draped in her white blanket all day. Each time someone would ask about it, her response was the same: "I'm practicing. I want to *become* my part for the play tonight."

I just chalked it up to another Princess Grace moment, but noticed too that I didn't seem quite as irritated with her as I might have earlier.

Gramma had brought a twenty-five-pound bag of sugar from her food storage (even a cupful was almost impossible to buy with the war shortages). She'd worked nonstop making Christmas treats for the neighbors and gingerbread men for the tree. The whole house smelled of candy, gingerbread, and spicy wassail.

I was placing one last cookie ornament on the tree when Dad walked in the door as the sun set. We grinned at each other as he held his finger to his lips for me to be quiet. Then hard and fast he shut the door and bellowed "Ho ho ho! Merry Christmas!" The windowpanes were still rattling as he placed his gray felt hat on the stand. Of course, the little ones all came running.

"Daddy, you are so late," said Dottie. As he lifted her, she patted his cheek.

"I've been busy shoveling at the church so we can find our way under all this snow," he said. "How's my little artist?" he poked her tummy.

I wished so much I could be little again, tucked in his arms where

I could whisper to him the Christmas-wish conflict in my heart. But it was Preston's turn. He was slopping kisses all over Dad's face by then. "What's all this?" said Dad.

"I'm giving you puppy kisses, like my new puppy who will find me for Christmas."

Dad held his finger to Preston's lips. "Did you forget? I'm going to pretend I didn't hear that, mister! Gramma's Christmas apron is the only place for wishes!" But Preston didn't seem worried. He kept kissing and puppy yelping.

Winnie came in with a gingerbread man all newly decorated. "Daddy, look what I've been doing. I'm making one for every person in the whole world!"

"Winnie, Winnie, you are wemarkable!" Dad said.

Winnie giggled. "I love to decorate."

"You do?" Dad said with a smile. Winnie had ribbons tied on each wrist, three in her hair, and one around each ankle.

"Hey, Pres," Dad said, "Millie needs some of your kisses." Preston wiggled away and, in an instant, he was planting a half dozen kisses on my face. His hands free again, Dad bent to pick up Georgie, who had toddled in, while at the same time admiring Winnie's decorating up close.

Will came running in. "Dad, Dad." He spread his arms as he turned in place. "See what Gramma built our house into." That was Will, always about building something.

"It's a Christmas wonderworld," added Winnie, jumping up and down.

"Wonderland!" Will corrected her. They began their typical twins' word war as they ran in circles.

"Wonderworld!"

"Wonderland!"

"Wonderworld!"

"Wonderland!"

The volume grew.

Grace joined the melee, her white robe still draped around her. "Such childish behavior." She waved her royal hand and stuck her nose in the air. I rolled my eyes toward Dad, and he chuckled under his breath.

"Hey. Indoor voices," Mom called from the kitchen, and the twins' jousting turned to whispers.

"Wonderworld."

"Wonderland."

"We only have an hour before we leave," Mom's voice continued, "and you aren't going to want to miss a minute of tonight's program."

"There's something very special happening this year!" Gramma chimed in.

"Millie, Gramma's helping to get Grace and me stage ready. Are you on board?" Mom called, moving to the bathroom.

"Don't worry, Mom. I'm on it." I stood to help the little ones get ready. Just then Gramma peeked her face around the corner to lift her eyebrow. "Thank you, Millie girl."

"Happy to, Gramma."

And I was. I was already dressed in my Sunday best myself, so I could help find matching socks, polish dress shoes, braid Winnie's wildfire hair and wrap up a box of her gingerbread men to take with us, iron Dottie's wrinkled sash, scrub mud off Will's pants, change Georgie's diaper, and more.

"Let's go." Dad's voice carried through the house. We gathered in the front room, pulling on coats and wrapping scarves.

"Doesn't my family look wonderful," said Mom.

"And you. You're going to steal the show," Dad said to Mom and Grace. They bowed. "Especially those silk stockings." Gramma had done a great job drawing a black line right up the back of Mom's legs to mimic the seam in real silk stockings. Dad whistled, and Mom smiled, ducking her head. We finally left for the church where, like every year since I was born, we would watch the Nativity reenacted and sing carols.

Hurrying down lamp-lit streets, we held hands to keep from slipping, except for Dad, who carried the big pot of wassail and a box of Winnie's cookies balanced on top.

Our town looked like a fairyland. The huge piles of snow glistened like hills of white jewels. Each pine bough held a heavy frosting, reminding me of the long tutus worn in our last ballet concert. We quickened our steps toward the warm glow of the double doors of the church and into the familiar building.

"Oh, pretty," we all seemed to say at once as we entered.

The stage was decorated in beautiful poinsettias, but they were white this year instead of red, placed on each step of the easy-access stairs flanking the outside of the stage.

While Mom and Grace climbed stage right and slipped behind the curtain, we made our way up front to the second row. The Gordons were just in front of us. They hadn't dressed up much, although Jimmy's hair was combed. Their smiles were warm as they turned to greet us. Their family seemed small without their dad—and no grandparents either. They weren't the only ones. There were so many families missing their dads and big brothers this Christmas, just like we were missing our grandpa.

Gramma held Georgie while Dad kept Winnie and Will from poking each other to death. I stared at my dad thinking I had the best father in the world. He didn't seem to care a smidge that Mom was getting all the attention tonight while he sat with the kids. *I picked the brightest star in the sky,* he would say. *How could I keep her from shining?*

I had Preston on my lap, sitting on the end in case he needed his usual trip to the drinking fountain. I was glad to be busy with him to help give my worry over Christmas wishes a rest.

We settled in as our church's pastor came on stage to welcome us. Everyone clapped. "We are grateful for all family members serving overseas," he said and gave a special salute—Gramma and others saluted back. Then the pastor said a prayer and with his "Amen," Mom came from behind the curtain. She was the narrator, as in years past. She had what Gramma called dignity and grace and was really talented. But instead of the limelight she had chosen us.

The lights dimmed, the curtains remained closed. Mom began. "And it came to pass . . ." Joseph came on stage, leading a donkey—a real donkey—with Mary on its back. A united whisper of "It's real . . ." rolled across the audience. Will and Winnie went crazy, pointing and bouncing. Dad put a gentle headlock around each twin head. They grinned up at him. Gramma, next to me, wasn't looking at the donkey or her daughter up there on stage; she was jostling and shushing baby Georgie, hoping he would fall asleep.

And that's when the connection came. I could see it in front of me, the lessons of family reaching generations back. Mom and Dad, Gramma and Grampa, Great-Gramma and Great-Grampa (the originators of the Christmas apron tradition)—all of them, like Mary and Joseph, made hard sacrifices for their children—for family.

I looked around. The audience was mesmerized by the scene and by Mom's soothing voice. Mesmerized, that is, until Preston, in his outdoor voice, said, "I want to ride the donkey." I winced. The whole audience chuckled. I knew mom had heard him. She didn't flinch, not even a blink.

Pointing to my lips to quiet Preston, I whispered in his ear. "Listen, Mommy's telling the story of baby Jesus." He quieted and snuggled into me.

Mom continued. "'And Joseph also went up from Galilee, out of the city of Nazareth, into Judæa, unto the city of David, which is called Bethlehem. . . . To be taxed with Mary his espoused wife, being great with child.'"

The familiar words sent chills through me. The audience sang "O Little Town of Bethlehem" while Joseph and Mary, dressed in colorful Nativity costumes, were—but for a flick of the donkey's tail—as still as a picture.

As the song ended, Joseph moved toward the innkeeper, now on stage. The innkeeper shook his head as Joseph asked for a room.

Joseph, Mary, and the donkey exited. Mom went on with the story we all knew so well. "'And there were . . . shepherds abiding in the field, keeping watch over their flock by night.'"

With colorful robes and headscarves and white stuffed lambs in their arms, the shepherds filled the apron of the stage, the deep blue velvet curtain their backdrop.

"'And, lo, the angel of the Lord came upon them.'"

Ever so slightly the curtains parted, and the shepherds moved aside to let an angel through. She pointed upward as if toward the star. A bright beam of light hit the stage. The shepherds' faces turned to look.

"'And the glory of the Lord shone round about them: and they were sore afraid. And the angel said unto them, Fear not: for, behold, I bring you good tidings of great joy, which shall be to all people. For unto you is born this day in the city of David a Saviour, which is Christ the Lord. And this shall be a sign unto you; Ye shall find the babe wrapped in swaddling clothes, lying in a manger.

"'And suddenly there was with the angel a multitude of the heavenly host . . .'"

Right in front of me there was movement. It was Jimmy Gordon's mom. She slipped off her coat, stood, and in a white angel costume, and, yes, silk stockings so well hidden before, she walked to the stage. In fact a host of angels stood in the audience, removed their overcoats, placed glittering halos on their heads, and glided as if on clouds to join the cast. The angels lined up two and three to a stair at each side of the stage.

"'. . . Praising God, and saying, Glory to God in the highest, and on earth peace, good will toward men.'"

The audience sang along with the angel choir, "Glory to God, Glory to God."

While we sang, the front of the stage and stairs emptied. Even Mom left, the curtain still closed.

We sang every verse through to the end. "Peace on earth, goodwill to men." There was a pause. Then the pianist began again. So we began again.

"Far, far away on Judea's plains, Shepherds of old heard the joyous strains: Glory to God . . ." We sang and sang and sang. Nothing on stage stirred. On our final, "Peace on earth, goodwill to men," we stopped. There was silence. Still nothing happened. Nothing. People began to whisper. Preston grabbed my face with his sweaty hands. But this time he knew to use his indoor voice.

"Let's go home!" he said.

"I don't think so." I whispered back while tickling his neck to distract him as we waited.

Then, ever so slowly, the curtains began to part. Center stage was the Nativity. The bright beam of light representing the star spread across the stage to engulf the whole scene. Mary, no longer great with child, sat by the manger, Joseph kneeling beside her. The donkey stood to the side of them. But this year was different; this year everything was white. Everything. Mary and Joseph had replaced colored robes and head drapes with white ones. The stable, the manger, the hay, everything—white. Pure white. Someone had even taken a white-wash to the donkey.

Mom returned in white and continued. "'And so it was, that, while they were there, the days were accomplished that she should be delivered. And she brought forth her firstborn son . . .'"

In walked angel Grace carrying a doll wrapped like the baby Jesus, a glittering halo in her white curls.

"'. . . And wrapped him in swaddling clothes, . . .'" Grace, in her royal way, handed the baby to Mary.

"'. . . And laid him in a manger; because there was no room for them in the inn.'" Angel Grace took her place on the risers above and behind the little family.

Shepherds, now in white, appeared from either side of the stage and then the wise men—all in white.

"'And they came with haste, and found Mary, and Joseph, and the babe lying in a manger.'" Everyone took a pose—motionless—creating a scene that looked like a life-sized white Nativity sculpture.

I felt a funny mix of surprise and peace, like I couldn't breathe or didn't need to. With the outside world peeled away, we were seeing into the heart of Christmas, into its true meaning—no outward show, just straight into the life-giving rhythmic pulse of our little town.

The audience sighed at the beautiful sight. The whole stage was frozen, as still as the outside winter, so still, and yet alive and bright under the light of the star of Bethlehem. White, on white, on white. Every face was turned toward the Christ child—every face but one. Grace was looking straight at the audience.

If anyone had noticed, they must have thought she looked a little daft, only one face looking out, all the rest doing as they had no doubt rehearsed. Yet she didn't look daft to me—not at all. I knew what was in Grace's heart. It wasn't about her being a princess after all. Although most of the audience sat in the dark, light from the stage fell on the first few rows. She was looking at her family. She wanted to see our faces as we saw the heart of Christmas, just like when she and I had taken the basket to the Gordons. What was the word she used? *Glorious.* Yes. Glorious.

"'For God so loved the world, that he gave his only begotten Son, that whosoever believeth in him should not perish, but have everlasting life.'" With Mom's final line: "On that silent night, holy night," we all stood to sing "Silent Night! Holy Night! All is calm, all is bright . . ."

There truly was a calm, bright feeling in the most important place pirouetting down through my whole soul. I understood. Christmas is what God and Jesus showed us how to do. Giving—sacrificing—a whole-soul gift so that someone else would have peace and joy. This was my answer. I knew what our family Christmas apron was all about—I knew what to do.

The song ended and everyone's eyes were damp. As the last tone of the piano faded, I came back to reality—the reality that Preston was no longer with me. He had slipped away and quick as a puppy made his way up to the stage. As he whizzed past, Mom nabbed him but was too late to cup her hand over his mouth as he blurted out,

"I wanna touch baby Jesus!" I waited for the audience to laugh, but instead of a chuckle, this time there was absolute stillness. Preston was speaking for all of us.

The feelings from that moment stayed with us as we ate Winnie's cookies and drank warm wassail, hugged and patted our neighbors and friends, and, with "Merry Christmas" farewells echoing in the air, made our way home. It was bedtime, three days before Christmas—the Gramma deadline. Time to make my wish.

* * *

Earlier that day, when I was still unsure, I had written out two slips. One read, 'A book—Millie.' With the family secret in mind, asking for something simple would make things easier for Mom and Dad. But now . . . it was the other wish, the one I held in my hand, that made sense. 'A horse for Grace—Millie.' I was so ready to trust in the true magic of family and Christmas and to believe that, somehow, Grace's whole-soul wish wasn't impossible after all.

Funny. My pink pointe shoe dream had all but faded. But my feet would keep dancing. I stood in the doorway. Across the living room the Christmas apron hung alone in the warm glow of the fire. I raised to relevé and, as silently as the sugarplum fairy and using the apron as my point to spot, counted chaînés, twenty tiny turns in all, before I stopped in front of it. Still high on the balls of my feet, I stayed balanced a long while remembering clear through the story of our family's first Christmas when that very apron had helped save Gramma's life as a baby.

With a new kind of hope, I lifted my hand and slipped the wish into the Christmas apron pocket, then let my hand hang empty and warm—clear up to my heart warm. My mind was quiet. I leaned my face against the apron. It soaked up my tears, like so many tears before.

The next three days were a blur. While Dad was at work Mom and Gramma were in constant motion. They made dozens of phone calls, ran errands, and visited neighbors. Between pie baking and divinity making Gramma showed us how to build a gingerbread house from scratch. Will was fascinated by the building, Winnie by the decorating, and Dottie made tiny little paintings to hang inside. And when Dad was home we were serenaded by Christmas carols in his Bing Crosby voice.

Grace and I were in charge of the younger ones, and each night neither one of us had a pinch of energy left for whispering after bedtime. Even so, the joy I felt as I made my Christmas wish was growing. A feeling that all was well—that whatever happened, I needn't worry.

* * *

Christmas Eve the family gathered as usual for caroling, Gramma's birthday cake, and the traditional telling of our family's first Christmas. We basked in the warm glow of the fire made even better by Gramma's story voice. We felt as safe, warm, and loved as Gramma must have felt her first day on earth. I moved my lips almost word for word with Gramma's.

That night bedtime didn't seem nearly as cold as past nights, and those usual feelings of irritation toward my princess sister had vanished. It seemed my head had just hit the pillow when suddenly it was Christmas morning.

* * *

The early sky was a frosty pink, and the smell of Gramma's cinnamon rolls filled the house. We children sat tucked together on the stairs waiting for Dad's permission to enter the magical room.

All seven of us were scrunched on the first two stairs. Georgie, wide-eyed and yawning, was sitting on my lap. Dottie squeezed up next to me, holding her hand over her own mouth, trying to stop the giggles. At my feet Preston kept tugging on my nightgown with the whisper, "Is it time yet?" Winnie and Will, in sprint stance, kept pulling each other back, determined to be the first. Grace, just below and to my right, was still and quiet, oddly not her princess self. She would catch my glance now and then, only to quickly look away.

At last came Dad's voice. "Come see your Christmas wishes come true!"

The whole group of us made the famous Christmas dash: arms reaching, mouths grinning, joy erupting as we ran to the tree, searched out our gift, and madly ripped away the only wrapping available—newspaper.

Winnie squealed. "The Christmas apron *is* magical. I got just what I asked for." Her box was stuffed with every color of hair ribbon.

"Me too!" said Dottie, waving paints and brushes.

"Now you can do art to fill up the whole house!" I said and got a hug.

Will was jumping all over as he squeezed his big tub of Lincoln Logs, and Preston hugged his wind-up puppy that could wag its own tail and bark.

"He seems to think it's real," whispered Gramma with a wink.

Meanwhile, Georgie ignored his little red ball, content with the newspaper he was busy ripping and wadding.

Only Grace and I were empty-handed. My heart sank. I couldn't help but look at Gramma as questions flashed in my head. Had I made the wrong wish? Had our family tradition lost its magic? I was happy enough for the younger ones. Maybe that's all that mattered. But what about Grace?

Hot tears formed, and I panicked a little just as Mom said, "Look here, behind the tree. This box has Millie's name on it, and here's one for Grace."

I wiped my tears on my nightgown sleeve, hoping no one had noticed, but knowing too that the gift Mom handed to Grace was definitely not a horse.

Everyone grew quiet as we opened the final gifts. I looked inside at the prettiest new pink pointe shoes I could ever have dreamed of. How could this be? Nobody had known . . . except . . . I looked at Grace. Her eyes told the story. Now full of tears of her own she was staring right at me.

"I can't believe it," Grace said. "I didn't think it was possible to find pointe shoes with a war going on . . . The apron *is* magic."

"You made *your* wish for *me?*" I was stunned, a tight feeling in my throat. I held the box close to me. "But what did *you* get, Grace?" The words came out raspy.

Still staring, eyes wide but not surprised, Grace absently tore at the paper of her package.

"I'm sorry I told, I . . . I had to see your face when you opened your wish, Mill."

Now I was staring at what was inside Grace's package.

A curry comb.

Grace seemed as puzzled as the other children and for one awful instant I thought, *Is this some kind of joke?*

Just then Gramma and Mom pointed toward our big front window. The younger ones gasped. Grace and I stared. Our mouths slowly opened.

There was Dad, atop a chestnut horse as big as any we had ever seen. Grace turned to me.

"You're the only one who knew, Millie. You gave your wish away for me, just like I did for you." Her whispering turned to a high soprano. "Oh, Millie. Thank you!" She threw her arms around me and I hugged her back just as tight.

Our show of gratitude was short-lived. Dad was motioning for us to come outside.

As we bundled everyone up, coats over pajamas, to welcome Grace's new pet, I took my time pulling on my boots and snow pants. When the others raced out, I stayed inside.

"I've got to hear this story," I said.

"Well," began Mom, "suffice it to say, there are angels in our little town. *That's* the magic that happened this Christmas. The gifts were rounded up and given with glad hearts because our town is filled with good people."

Gramma jumped in. "And because even when there isn't much to spare, your parents are always thinking of others, not only during hard times. The dozens of loaves of bread your mom has delivered over the years, your dad's willingness to help whenever someone's in need—shoveling, fixing cars . . ."

"Ah." I thought back to the basket for the Gordons. "Loaves and fishes. Well, I can understand all of that, but pointe shoes and a horse in the middle of a war, and no money?" The long-held secret I had resented hearing and keeping was finally out. No one even seemed to notice.

"Oh, the horse *was* remarkable," Mom said. "Mr. Henderson is moving to the city for a year and when he heard we were looking— well, remember when Dad helped him build the addition to his house last summer?—He was delighted his horse could be taken care of by 'family.' He's even having a load of hay and a couple bags of oats delivered. And a year's plenty long enough. Who knows what will be in Grace's head by next Christmas."

We all smiled.

Mom continued. "Then there was a little problem of where to keep such a large animal, so Gramma talked to Mrs. Gordon. She was happy to keep our new pet penned in their pasture. 'Anything for your children,' Mrs. Gordon said. 'They've been so good to our Jimmy.'"

"And the pointe shoes?" I asked.

"Let's just say Mistress Allen thinks the world of her star pupil and would go to the ends of the earth to get you ready for *The Nutcracker* next year."

A definite lump in my throat kept me in silence for a while.

"So." Words finally squeaked out. "We all got our whole-soul wish."

"Especially me," said Gramma.

"Oh, and by the way, Millie," Mom said, "where all these gifts came from is a secret."

"All of us already know, Mom. It's the apron. The apron is the symbol of family. Aprons help us do the most important work there is—family work. The work that says 'I love you.'" Repeating their own words to the two women who had taught me the most seemed to startle them a bit.

"No doubt you'll have a Christmas apron for your own family, Millie girl," said Gramma.

"I hope so, Gramma. I hope so." She wiped tears away as I hugged her tight.

Not wanting to miss the excitement any longer, I buttoned my coat and ran outside. Dad hoisted me on top of the horse to squeeze in with the others. I held baby Georgie in my arms. It wasn't exactly the fairytale horse Grace had described, but it was perfect for our family. That horse's back was large enough to seat us all, one after the other. We hung on tight to each other as Dad led Grace's horse around the yard. When we headed off toward the Gordons' pasture, Gramma called to us. We looked back, and there she was on the porch smiling and waving the Christmas apron.

"Happy birthday, Gramma," we said together. I leaned up past the little ones sitting between us and said, "Grace, what are you going to name her?"

"That's easy," said Grace as she turned back to look me right in the face. "Her name is Dancer."

About the Author

Photo by Nicole Carman Christensen

Rachelle Pace Castor grew up with a rich heritage in family, God, and the arts. She is a lover of people and their stories. She writes mostly of the journey of the heart, and believes that people are innately good, kind, and compassionate. "It's our lives' passages, especially in relationships, that help us remember our eternal identity. My hope in recording 'goodness' through story is to plant deep in the heart of the reader this truth—it is our loving choices that give humans unending strength, a dusting of deity." To learn more about *The Christmas Apron,* please visit www.thechristmasapron.net.

RACHELLE PACE CASTOR EXTENDS HEARTFELT APPRECIATION . . .

Voices of my many mothers and grandmothers harmonize throughout *The Christmas Apron.* Above all the rest I thank my mother, Diane, and her mother, Karolla, whom I long to be like. Others I honor for their part in tutoring me through genes and generations: Rosa May, Hannah Caroline, Phoebe, Sylvia Annette, Sylvia, Little Grandma Wise, and some whom I have yet to meet, including my father's mother, Agnes, who, from the stories, undoubtedly still wears her apron well.

I thank also women who may not know I count them as "Mother": Joan, Bonnie, Rachel, JoAn, Kathy, Mary, Pat, and Ione. Thank you for showing me what matters most.

And particularly to Janet, who with grace and art has woven through so many of our lives the joy of creating family symbols, including one spring evening when she revealed the simple beauty of her apron collection, the inspiration for this tale.

And finally to my father, who through a lifetime of selfless acts, received for his family a well-deserved portion of loaves and fishes as he sat atop a huge chestnut horse outside our front-room window the Christmas of my sister's whole-soul wish.

I love you all.